The Blood Binding
A Belldonna Johnson Adventure

The Blood Binding

HELEN STRINGER

For my father

I.

The Spirits of the Black Waters

IT WAS RAINING again. Belladonna hunkered down in her seat and watched the buildings slide by through the greasy, rain-spattered windows. The windows on school trip buses were always greasy, from sticky fingers and foreheads and heaven knew what else.

Belladonna didn't want to speculate. It was too icky.

They were on another one of Mr. Watson's history trips. This time it was some Roman ruin near the coast. The jagged remains of a fort near what had been a port, but had long since silted up into one of those endless beaches where you couldn't even see the ocean at low tide.

There had been a time when Belladonna had loved trips to the seaside, even when it rained. Sometimes, those were the best trips of all. Her dad would park the car as close to the roaring waves as possible and they'd sit and eat cold sausages and hard-boiled eggs and drink tea from a thermos while the seagulls circled over the grey, roiling water.

But the prospect of a freezing plod around some low stone walls and a makeshift museum didn't excite quite the same feelings.

The bus slowed and turned into a small gravel parking lot.

"Right!" said Watson. "You've all got your worksheets. I know it's a bit wet, but we'll see what we can do."

He glanced at his watch.

"A *bit* wet," said Steve, suddenly appearing next to Belladonna's seat. "We don't need a bus, we need a bleeding ark."

Belladonna couldn't help smiling, but Mr. Watson was already herding everyone off.

"Half an hour to look around the fort! Then everyone into the museum for lunch and a talk from the museum director! Got that?"

There were a few mumbled "yes sirs," but most of his charges just pushed their way off the bus and scattered across the landscape.

Belladonna zipped up her jacket, pulled the hood up, hoisted her pink backpack onto one shoulder and stepped off the bus.

The place looked utterly miserable. The sky was the color of lead and the clouds were so low, they seemed to push down on her already dismal spirits. For some reason, her mum and dad had hardly been around. They were there when she got up in the morning and came home at night, but her mum hadn't cooked anything for weeks and her grandmother had brought dinner every evening instead, which meant buying things in boxes from the local supermarket and microwaving them when she got there, so that even the beef vindaloo they'd had the night before had tasted vaguely of cardboard.

She trudged to the far side of the parking lot and started with what had been the parade ground, a flat expanse of earth that the Romans had used for training. She half expected to see a phantom cohort marching up and down, but there was nothing – just muddy grass and a small raised area where the commanders had stood and watched their men.

She strolled across the parade ground and up onto the platform. What must it have been like for the soldiers, she wondered. Mr. Watson had explained that many of the Roman legions were made up of men from the far reaches of the empire, not necessarily those from Italy. But she couldn't help thinking that when you looked at maps of the Empire, most of it seemed to be in fairly warm places, like the Mediterranean, the middle east and north Africa. Getting posted to the north of England really must have felt like getting the fuzzy end of the lollipop.

She turned to leave the mound, but slipped on the wet grass and skidded down the side, landing with a thump.

"Great," she thought. *"Typical!"*

She scrambled to her feet, brushed herself off, and was just thinking that at least no one had seen her, when the unmistakable sound of giggling skittered across the grass.

She spun around, hoping against hope that it wasn't

Sophie Warren or any of her minions, but it wasn't anyone she recognized.

It was a girl with reddish hair, sitting on the railway ties that bounded the parking lot. Belladonna glowered at her, then stopped. This wasn't one of her classmates. She wasn't wearing a jacket, for one thing, and she wasn't clutching a copy of Mr. Watson's worksheets, for another.

Belladonna hesitated for a moment, then walked toward her. As she got closer, she could see that the girl was the same age as her, or maybe a little younger. She was very thin and completely sodden. Her reddish hair was plastered to her head and hung in dank rattails down her back, half sticking to the sides of her face, and the worn garland that crowned her head seemed sad, rather than festive. Her dress was little more than a simple shift, and had probably been white at one time, but was now the color of mud.

Belladonna glanced around to make sure no one was near.

"Hello," she said, softly.

The girl looked surprised, and instinctively turned around, as if she thought there must be someone standing behind her.

"No," said Belladonna. "I said hello to you."

"You can see me?" whispered the girl.

"Yes. You laughed at me."

The girl stared at her for a moment before a smile spread across her grubby face.

"You looked funny. Your legs and arms all went in

different directions."

"I'm Belladonna."

"Branwyn," whispered the girl.

She fingered at her leather necklace and smiled.

"That looks tight," said Belladonna. "Why don't you take it off?"

Branwyn looked confused.

"What?"

"Your necklace. It looks uncomfortable."

"Johnson! What the devil are you doing over there?"

Mr. Watson stomped across the parking lot.

"The fort is over there," he said, pointing to the walls.

"Yes, but this is the parade ground," said Belladonna, turning to the page on the worksheet. "We're supposed to mark it off, see?"

"Yes, mark it off, not set up camp. You know students aren't supposed to wander off alone."

"Yes, sir."

"Right, well. Get on with it, then."

He marched off. Belladonna glanced at Branwyn and was surprised to see that she had shrunken back, an expression of fear on her face.

"Is he your Seer?" she whispered, her voice shaking slightly.

"Our…? No, he's just Mr. Watson, our teacher. I'd better do as he says, though."

Branwyn smiled uncertainly.

"It was nice meeting you," said Belladonna, a little awkwardly. It was always a bit hard to end conversations with ghosts, as if you were abandoning them, somehow.

Branwyn smiled briefly, brushing her hair away from her face, which didn't help her general appearance one bit.

"I haven't spoken to anyone in a long time," she whispered. "It was nice. I'm always here if you'd like to talk again."

Belladonna couldn't tell her that the bus trip had taken over an hour and that it was very unlikely she'd be able to return, but she just nodded, turned, and made her way across the parking lot to the maze of low stone walls, roughly sculpted horse troughs and stacks of tiles from the ancient hypocausts.

She finished her worksheet and joined everyone else as they headed toward the small museum for lunch, though she couldn't help glancing back to see if Branwyn was still sitting on the edge of the parade ground.

She was.

"What is it?" asked Steve, his voice low and his attitude nonchalant, so that no one would think he was actually talking to the weird girl. "A ghost?"

"Yeah, but…"

"But what?"

"There's something odd."

"Is it a soldier?"

"No. A girl."

Steve grunted and melted away into the crush of kids trying to get through the single narrow door into the museum.

Mr. Watson led the way to a small cafeteria, where everyone sat down and got out whatever sandwiches and drinks they had brought for lunch. Belladonna usually had some strange concoction assembled by her mother, but this time it was just a store-bought ham sandwich in a plastic wrapper with a bottle of fizzy orange instead of Tizer.

Toward the end of lunch the museum director arrived and introduced herself as Dr. Hartley. She was short and rather round, with cropped grey hair, green wellington boots, and a pair of glasses on a string around her neck. She told them the history of the fort and how the land where it was built had once been marshland and peat bog and that the Romans had built the ground up so it was solid enough to hold the stone fort.

Mr. Watson had covered most of this in class and Belladonna's mind began to wander to the girl outside. She looked out of the window and could just make her out through the rain, still sitting in the same place.

Then it came to her.

The girl was soaked through.

But she was a ghost. The rain shouldn't touch her. Not here in the Land of the Living.

"...it was thought that the body dated from this period. A theory that was confirmed by an examination of the seeds and plants found with it."

"What?" thought Belladonna. *"Why do people only say interesting things when I'm not listening?"*

"Thank you, Dr. Hartley, that was very informative," said Mr. Watson, standing. "I'm sure everyone is very grateful to you for taking the time to describe the museum's work."

He glanced sharply at the class, who had been on enough trips by now to know that what was expected at this point was applause.

"Good," said Watson, clearly pleased. "You've got an hour and a half to spend in the museum. Don't forget to identify something that interests you the most, draw a picture of it, make notes and be prepared to talk about it in class next week."

There was the usual murmured assent as lunches were packed away and clumps of kids meandered off into the maze of small rooms that made up the museum.

Belladonna caught up with Lucy Fisher, who was dropping her egg salad sandwiches into the bin. Lucy's mum always made her egg salad sandwiches for school trips, but Lucy never ate them. She wolfed down the regular school dinners, so Belladonna could only guess that it was the egg salad she didn't like. Once, she'd mentioned that Lucy should perhaps tell her mum, an idea that Lucy had greeted with a look of total incredulity, as if Belladonna had suggested sticking her hand down the waste disposal, which only confirmed what Belladonna had always thought: other people's families were weird. Which was quite something when she considered that her family consisted of two ghosts, a psychic grandma (who wasn't really psychic), and an aunt who was off somewhere chasing down the Wild Hunt.

"Lucy," she said. "What was that stuff about a body?"

"Weren't you listening?" asked Lucy.

"Of course I wasn't listening," thought Belladonna. *"Why else would I ask?"*

She didn't say it out loud, though. Lucy was so timid she made Belladonna look like the class clown.

"No...I was sort of daydreaming. Was it a Roman soldier?"

"It was a girl," said Lucy, her voice low as if it were some big secret, rather than something the entire class had been told only minutes before. "Isn't that creepy? They found her in the peat bog and it turned out she was over two thousand years old!"

Belladonna and Lucy made their way through the museum. Some things were boring, but others were fascinating. There were the remains of sandals worn by soldiers and delicate shoes worn by the camp commander's wife. They'd even found some letters in which she had invited the wife of another camp commander over for a birthday celebration.

As they walked into the last room, there was a buzz of excitement. Most of the kids seemed to be lingering there, leaning over a glass case, mesmerized.

Belladonna eased her way through the crowd, Lucy following in her wake. When they got to the case, Lucy winced.

"Oh, that's awful! That's awful!" She turned away and pushed back through the crowd.

"It's amazing, isn't it?" said Steve. He was standing on the other side of the case and was clearly fascinated.

"I'm...I don't..."

"It's because the peat's anaerobic," said Steve. "That means there's almost no oxygen, so a body buried in peat doesn't decay. Not even the hair or the stitches on their clothing."

"How d'you know that?" asked Rob, a sturdy boy who, as long as Belladonna had known him, had never listened to a word in class or cracked open a single book. He was good at football, though, which seemed to make up for everything else.

"I have a book about the Bog People at home," said Steve, his words coming fast and betraying his fascination. "They've found them all over the place, Ireland, the Netherlands, Germany, and here. Mostly they're adults, but some of them are children."

"It's gruesome," said Philippa Lawler, wrinkling her nose. "I've never seen anything like it. Have you, Belladonna?"

Belladonna stared at the thing in the case. It was a little twisted, distorted from the weight of two thousand years of peat, and not all of it was there, but there was no mistaking the simple dress, the reddish hair and, above all, the garland of flowers that circled her head.

She backed away from the case, hoping that she looked like she'd just seen enough and was going to look at the tile samples, but as she turned she saw Steve staring at her. He followed her back out to the cafeteria.

"What is it?"

"It's her. The girl in the parking lot. That's why she's still wet."

"What?"

"That's what was odd. It's raining, but she's a ghost. She shouldn't be wet."

"But she was wet when she died."

Belladonna nodded.

"Can you see her? Over there." She pointed toward the parade ground.

"I don't know," said Steve, squinting into the rain. "It's been a while."

Belladonna brushed her hand against his.

"Whoa! Yes! But what is she doing there? It's miserable. Why doesn't she just go to the Land of the Dead. Why would she want to stay where it…where it happened?"

"Let's go ask her," said Belladonna, heading for the door.

Steve glanced back into the museum reluctantly.

"It's okay," said Belladonna. "I'll just say I dropped something when I was over there and Mr. Watson said we aren't supposed to go anywhere alone."

"We've used that one before, Belladonna. We're going to have to come up with something new one day."

Belladonna grinned, pulled up her hood and stepped out into the rain. Steve followed, though his hoodie wasn't much protection from the downpour. They hadn't gone far before she slowed down and looked at him.

"What d'you mean 'where it happened?' Where what happened?"

Steve stopped.

"They think…archaeologists and stuff…they think…that is, they're fairly sure that…that the people found in the bogs were sacrificed."

"Sacrificed?"

"Maybe when food was scarce or something. They'd

give them some kind of drugged drink--"

"Wait. How do they know that?"

"They've found the remains in some of the stomachs. Anyway, they'd drug them, then take them out to the marshes and strangle them. Sometimes they'd cut their throats, too."

"Strangle them?" Belladonna's blood ran cold.

"Yeah, and…what's wrong?"

"I thought it was a necklace. I told her it looked tight."

"Well, it probably is," said Steve. "Come on, let's find out why she's still here."

They trudged across the ruins to the parking lot and over to where Branwyn waited, smiling and clearly pleased to see Belladonna again.

"Hello!"

"Hello, Branwyn. This is my friend Steve."

"Hello, Steve."

"Branwyn…we were wondering, why are you here?"

"Why I'm here?"

"Yes," said Steve. "You do know you're dead, right?"

"Yes," whispered Branwyn sadly, her hand flittering to the leather band around her neck.

"Ow!" yelped Steve, clutching at his chest.

Belladonna and Branwyn stared at him.

"What is it?"

"It's…something sharp." He reached into his jacket and pulled out a small blade with an elaborate hilt.

Branwyn shrank back.

"No," she whispered. "Please. They promised they wouldn't do that. They promised!"

"The Rod of Gram?"

Steve nodded and leaned forward. He tried to steady Branwyn with his left hand, but it passed right through her.

"I don't see how…" he started.

"The strap, try just the strap," said Belladonna.

Branwyn was weeping now, her ghostly tears leaving trails of pale skin in their wake.

"Please…"

Steve leaned down again, reached for the strap and sliced through it. He unwound it gently from around Branwyn's neck and stepped back. The strap immediately crumbled into dust and blew away on a gust of wind as the blade returned to its usual form—a somewhat battered plastic six-inch ruler.

Belladonna had to admit that there was a part of her that hoped it was the leather thong that had held Branwyn to the spot where she died, but if her experiences with the dead had taught her anything, it was that things were seldom so simple.

"Can you go now?" she asked, hoping against hope.

"Go where?" asked Branwyn, puzzled.

"To the Land of the Dead," said Steve. "The Other Side. It's really nice. The weather's a *lot* better."

Branwyn looked from one to the other in disbelief, as if she'd stumbled upon the stupidest people on the planet.

"I can't go," she whispered. "I can't go anywhere."

"Why not?" asked Belladonna.

"And what's with the whispering?" asked Steve.

13

"If I whisper they stay away," she said. "Can't you see them? They're all around!"

Steve looked at Belladonna. She nodded and closed her eyes, feeling the strength of the Words as they came to her lips. But this time they weren't quite so strange, this time they were Words she had used before.

"*Igi si gar*," she said, then again, louder. "*Igi si gar*!!"

Reveal yourself!

"Oh, sh…criminy!!!" Steve staggered back, falling over the railroad ties and landing in the gravel.

Belladonna opened her eyes. He was staring at something, and from the angle of his gaze, it was something very big.

And it was behind her.

She turned around slowly. It wasn't an "it," it was a them: huge swirling, morphing black clouds, like giant murmurations of starlings. Belladonna stared. They were almost beautiful, but the waves of menace that pulsed across the parade ground and parking lot prevented them from being anything other than terrifying.

"Steve…"

"I know! I know!" Steve scrambled to his feet and pulled out the ruler, but instead of turning into something useful, he found himself holding something he'd never seen before. "What's that?" he said, staring at it.

"It's a pair of secateurs," said Belladonna, glancing sideways but unwilling to take her eyes off the swirling black clouds.

"A pair of *what*??"

"Secateurs," repeated Belladonna. "They're used for

gardening. My mum had some."

"*Gardening???*"

"What are they?" asked Belladonna.

"Spirits of the Black Water," said Branwyn. "They destroy crops, spread disease, bring death to animals and men. We had to keep them here."

"Here?"

"Here where the black water is. Our Seers would bind them to the peat marsh. That's why I cannot leave, even if I wanted to."

"Wait…" Steve glanced at Branwyn, unwilling to take his attention away from the swirling masses of whatever-it-was that surrounded them. "They used *you*? *You're* the one who is keeping them here?"

"Blood binds strongest."

"But…you're dead," said Steve. "You don't have any blood. Your body isn't even here, it's over there in the museum."

"I think you might be being too literal," said Belladonna.

"I don't know what that means," said Branwyn.

"It means it's not actual blood. It's the kind where… you know, when people describe someone as a 'blood relative.' It just means they're related."

"Yes," Branwyn said, smiling. "That's it. But it couldn't be him, could it? He was too important. I didn't matter. I was a girl and I had a limp. No one would ever take me to wife. It was all explained."

"By who?" said Steve.

"Whom," said Belladonna.

15

"Whatever. It was the Seer, wasn't it? Was he your father?"

"No. My father died of the ague. My uncle had been bound here before, but it turned out my grandmother yielded to temptation and he was not of the blood."

"Good for granny," muttered Steve.

"So the Seer was your grandfather?"

"My great-uncle. They said he was the greatest seer that had ever been. He was the only one who knew how to bind the Spirits of the Black Water."

"I bet he did," said Steve, his voice dripping with sarcasm.

"But there must be something we can--"

"There isn't," said Branwyn. "This is how things must be. But thank you for spending some time with me. And thank you very much for removing the band. I feel much better now."

"But..." began Belladonna.

Steve took her arm and pulled her away. The secateurs returned to the shape of the ruler and the shifting Spirits became more faint.

"We have to do something," said Belladonna, wrenching her arm free. "We can't just leave her like this!"

"I know," said Steve. "But we're not going to figure it out here, are we? We need to find out more. Find out exactly what those things are."

Belladonna wanted him to be wrong, wanted some Words to come, but she knew that they wouldn't. This was something else, something as old as the Earth, something even older than the Queen of the Abyss.

"We'll be back," she yelled. "Branwyn, we'll help you, I promise."

Branwyn turned, smiled and waved, watching as they walked before returning to her lonely vigil, keeping the Spirits of the Black Water bound and idly picking pieces of peat from her red hair.

2.

Cradoe

THE BACK OF THE BUS was as noisy as ever on the trip back to school, but Belladonna couldn't help noticing that, for once, Steve wasn't at the epicenter of things. He was sitting next to the window on the back seat, lost in thought.

The short October days meant that it was nearly dark by the time they got back, and the streets around the school were clogged with the cars of parents unwilling to let their kids find their own ways home through the gloomy streets. The ones who did have to walk left quickly, while there was still a faint glimmer of day. The rain had stopped, though, so things weren't quite as dreary as they might have been.

Steve took a back way and met Belladonna a couple of blocks away from the school. Ever since the incident with the Proctors and the standing stones, Miss Parker had insisted that, as Paladin, it was part of his job to make sure the Spellbinder got home safely. He had agreed, but wasn't prepared to go so far as to let anyone see him doing it.

On most days he would jump out of the bushes and try to scare her, but today he just fell into step beside her as they made their way to Lychgate Lane. Belladonna glanced at him through the dark curtains of her lank hair. There was something unsettling in his silence.

"What is it?" she said, finally.

Steve shrugged and they walked on in silence until the black spire of St. Abelard's came into view.

"It's just…" he said, suddenly. "She's…I mean, she *was* about our age, wasn't she?"

"Yes, I think so."

"What would it have been like?"

"To die like that, you mean?"

"Yes. No. Sort of." He stopped and looked over at the silhouettes of the gravestones in the cemetery. "Everyone goes eventually. Even kids. We could get sick or have an accident…"

"Or get beheaded by a huge faceless demon."

"Yeah," said Steve, remembering the Allu and smiling. "That too. But it's not the same as someone from your own family walking up to you and telling you that they're going to take you into some swamp and strangle you, is it?"

"No. And telling her that she'd been chosen not because she was special, but because she was worthless."

"D'you think they did it in the dark?"

Belladonna shuddered.

"Don't think about it," she said. "It's too awful. We'll go and see Miss Parker in the morning."

"Okay."

They walked on up the street until the lights of 65 Lychgate Lane could be clearly seen.

"See you tomorrow then," said Steve.

"'Bye," said Belladonna.

But he was already gone, running down the street and around the corner. Belladonna walked up the path and opened the door.

"I'm home!" she shouted.

"We're in the kitchen!"

It was Grandma Johnson's voice. That meant frozen food for dinner again.

Belladonna dumped her bag by the door and hung her anorak on its hook before dawdling into the kitchen.

"Hey, kiddo!" said her dad, cheery as ever. "How were the Roman ruins?"

"Wet. Where's mum?"

"She's busy, Belladonna. Come on, sit down and get those wet shoes off."

A chair moved itself out from the table and Belladonna sat down and leaned over to take off her shoes. Which was when she noticed the glance that her dad and Grandma Johnson exchanged. She sat up and looked at them, suddenly worried.

"What is it? What's happened?"

"Nothing," said Grandma Johnson, softly. "Everything's fine. She's just busy."

She turned to her dad.

"Really," he said. "D'you think I'd be here if she wasn't alright?"

"Yes, but--"

"She's not your Aunt Deirdre," said Grandma Johnson, almost reading her thoughts. "She hasn't gone off on some wild goose chase. She's on the Other Side... busy."

Belladonna felt somewhat reassured, but she still didn't like the situation, and she liked it even less when, after dinner, her dad dematerialized before the credits of "Staunchly Springs" had even finished.

"Don't you have any homework?" asked Grandma Johnson.

"Yes."

"Well then."

Belladonna went out to the hall, grabbed her bag and stomped up the stairs to her room. She whizzed through the math homework without her usual care, then skimmed the chapter of "Silas Marner" they were supposed to read for English. She usually liked English, but "Silas Marner" was without doubt *the* most boring book on the face of the planet.

She grabbed a stack of books about mythology through the ages and went back downstairs. The school secretary, Mrs. Jay, had given a set each to her and Steve with instructions to memorize everything. It had been interesting at first, but after a while all the creatures, gods, goddesses and demons had started to sort of meld together and she'd stopped reading them.

She was still a little annoyed about no one telling her

what was going on with her mum, but when she got downstairs the living room fire was on and Grandma Johnson had made hot chocolate and put three packets of Parma Violets on a plate. Belladonna sat on the floor near the fire and felt bad about the stomping. She sipped her hot chocolate , munched some Parma Violets, and began leafing through the books.

Now she wished she'd stuck at it longer when she'd first been given them. There were four books, and each was about four inches thick—it was like hunting for a needle in a haystack. No…worse…it was like looking for a particular needle in a stack of needles. She turned the pages of each and then checked the indexes.

"What are you looking for, dear?"

"Spirits of the Black Water," said Belladonna.

She told her grandmother about Branwyn and the strange, malevolent clouds.

"And that's what she called them? Spirits of the Black Water?"

"Yes, but they're not mentioned in any of these books and Mrs. Jay said she'd never heard of them either."

"Well, don't worry dear, I'm sure Miss Parker will know what to do. Now drink your chocolate milk, it's time for that alien autopsy show."

"You know that UFO stuff is all rubbish, right Grandma? It's not real."

"Yes, well that's what most people say about ghosts, isn't it? Have another Parma Violet and change the telly to channel five."

The next morning the rain was back and even with all the lights on, the classrooms at Dulworth's seemed cloaked in gloom. French seemed to drag on forever, with Madame Huggins going on and on about irregular verbs, which appeared to be nearly all of them, as far as Belladonna could make out. Then came geography with Mr. Kettlewick. They were doing North America, but Belladonna couldn't concentrate on what he was saying because he kept pronouncing the Appalachians as Appa-latch-ianze, when she'd seen a documentary just last week and knew it was supposed to be Appa-laysh-anz.

When break finally rolled around, she met Steve at the foot of the stairs that led to the science labs and Miss Parker's office. They practically ran to her door and pressed the buzzer.

"I never thought I'd actually *want* to come and see old Parker," said Steve.

"Sh!" said Belladonna. "She'll hear you!"

Silence. No red busy light, no yellow wait light and no green enter light.

"She was in assembly," said Belladonna. "She *has* to be here."

She pressed the buzzer again. Silence.

Steve turned the door handle.

"Steve! You can't do that!"

He smiled, pushed the door open a crack and stuck his head inside.

"Rats and earwigs!"

"What?"

"Look," he said, flinging the door wide.

Belladonna glanced around the landing, nervously, making sure no one was watching, then cautiously stepped into the office.

Her heart sank. It wasn't just that Miss Parker wasn't there—the lacrosse stick she kept mounted on the wall was missing too. The stick became her staff when she was the Queen of the Abyss, the ruler of the Land of the Dead, and the fact that it was not in its frame could mean only one thing.

"Oh, no! She's on the Other Side!"

"We could ask Mrs. Jay," suggested Steve. "She gave us all those mythology books, after all."

"*What* do you *think* you are doing?" boomed an all-too-familiar voice behind them. "And ask me what?"

"I'm sorry," stammered Steve. "We were…that is…"

"We wanted to ask Miss Parker about the Spirits of the Black Waters."

"About the what?"

Mrs. Jay hustled them back into Miss Parker's office and closed the door.

"Explain," she snapped.

Steve told her about Branwyn and the huge black shifting clouds.

Mrs. Jay listened carefully, thought for a moment, then shook her head.

"Never heard of them."

"Then where--" began Belladonna.

Mrs. Jay silenced her with a shake of her head.

"You can't help every ghost that's in trouble," she said. "That's not why you're here. There are always going to be unfortunate situations. You are here to prevent the Empress of the Dark Spaces returning. You should be learning the skills that you will need on that dark day and finding the nomials that will form the Multiversal Orrery. These spirits, or whatever they are, have already been bound. They pose no danger. Now get back downstairs, break is nearly over."

She pushed them out of the office, closed the door and then locked it.

"But we can't just--"

"Yes, you can. Now go!"

They walked down the stairs slowly and were met by a familiar figure waiting near the hot drinks machine.

"What-ho, chums!" said Elsie, cheerily.

"Oh, great," muttered Steve.

"Where have you been?" asked Belladonna. "We haven't seen you for ages."

"Oh, everyone's getting ready for the parties," said Elsie, her perfect chestnut curls, bouncing with excitement.

"What parties?"

"Halloween, of course," said Elsie, as if it were the most obvious thing in the world. "It's tomorrow!"

"And the ghosts have parties?"

"Yes. Lots of them."

"Since when?" asked Steve, skeptically.

"Since always," said Elsie. "Well, not last year, obviously. All that Dr. Ashe stuff put rather a damper on things. Speaking of dampers, why so glum?"

Belladonna told the story of Branwyn yet again,

finishing just as the bell sounded for the end of break and the halls suddenly filled with students on their way to classes.

"Hmm," said Elsie, thoughtfully. "I'll see what I can find out. Library later?"

"Yes," said Steve. "Lunchtime."

Elsie nodded and vanished.

"See you later," muttered Steve, strolling away and disappearing into the crowd.

Belladonna sighed and made her way to the other end of the school and double chemistry. The rest of the morning stretched on endlessly, and even the fact that Steve still managed to make his solution go "bang!" when it was just supposed to turn purple didn't really help matters much. Mr. Morris didn't even send him to see Miss Parker, he just made a slight huffing noise and moved on to Sophie Warren, whose solution was just the right color...of course.

"I almost wouldn't mind her constantly picking on me if she could just get a "D" in something once in while," complained Belladonna when they reached the solitude of the small, almost entirely useless library.

"I think I need to expand my repertoire," said Steve. "Move on from loud noises. Smells, maybe."

"Don't," said Belladonna, wrinkling her nose. "It'd get in everyone's hair and clothes."

Steve grinned in a way that was always worrying to anyone that knew him.

"Hey," he said. "I think I might have figured out why no one's heard of the Spirits of the Black Water."

"Why?"

"Well, I was looking at my book about the bog people..."

"When?"

"In the back of chemistry. Double lessons are so boring. So I was reading the book and it said that nobody knows much about the culture of the bog people because they don't seem to have had a system of writing."

"I've heard that before," said Belladonna, hoping that Steve couldn't see how impressed she was. "I saw a documentary about druids and stuff and it said they passed everything down by word of mouth."

"Right, which would explain why no one's heard of their gods or their demons. Once the last member of the tribe, or whatever, died out, it was gone forever."

"Except it isn't," said Elsie, materializing near the classics, and looking more than usually pleased with herself.

"It isn't?" said Belladonna.

Elsie glanced to her left and looked vaguely annoyed.

"Come on," she said, a little impatiently, to what appeared to be nothing. "It'll be fine. They're nice, I promise."

They stared at the space next to Elsie and slowly, slowly, a dark form began to take shape. From Elsie's tone of voice, Belladonna had been expecting it to be a child, but it was a grown man, small and muscular and very nervous.

"It's the first time he's been back in over two thousand

years," explained Elsie. "He doesn't have very good memories of the place."

By the time he'd finished materializing, Belladonna found herself looking at a man with fine features and a broad brow. He was wearing a simple leather top and trousers that looked like they were made of the same rough-woven material as Branwyn's dress. His hair was brown and raggedly cut, and much of his body was stained with complex whorls and patterns by some kind of dye. But the most striking thing about him was the look of inconsolable sorrow on his face.

"This is Belladonna and Steve," explained Elsie. "Steve, Belladonna, this is Cradoe, Branwyn's uncle."

Belladonna had heard people talk about being so surprised that their jaw dropped, but this was the first time she actually experienced it.

"Seriously?" said Steve. "This is really…wow."

"The lady Elsie tells me that you have seen my niece and that she is still bound."

"Yes. I'm sorry."

"And the Spirits of the Black Water. They are still there?"

"Yes," said Belladonna. "We saw them. Branwyn said that was why she couldn't leave. That she was part of the binding."

"She spoke the truth."

Belladonna's heart sank. It looked like Mrs. Jay was right. There really are some things that can't be fixed.

"And…?" said Elsie. "Tell them what you told me."

"He lied," said Cradoe quietly. "Riagan lied to us all.

It did not need to be a blood binding. He just wanted to rid himself of those who were most favored of our Pennaeth."

"Your what?"

"Our…leader, the chieftain of our people."

"But…what threat could Branwyn have been? She was just a girl."

"She was the last. I was told by those that came when their time was run, that he broke the binding of my blood himself, but let it be known that my mother had not been true and that was why my blood was impure. It was untrue, but she was cast out and sent across the shifting sands to die."

"Yikes," said Steve. "You guys were strict!"

"You said the binding could be done without blood," said Belladonna. "Can you tell us how? Could we free her?"

"I don't know if she can be freed, but I can tell you the charm," said Cradoe, sadly. "So much time has passed."

Belladonna pulled a notebook and pen out of her bag.

"Right," she said. "Fire away."

"What?"

"They speak strangely sometimes," explained Eslie.

"Pots and kettles," muttered Steve.

"She wants you to tell them the charm."

"It is the Nine Herbs Charm," said Cradoe. "But with two additions. The Spirits of the Black Waters must be bound with eleven."

"The Nine Herbs Charm?" Belladonna looked at him. "I'm sorry, we don't know…"

"You do not know the Charm of Nine? But how do you treat your sick or those poisoned by sorcery?"

"We use the Charm of Antibiotics," said Steve.

"And that is a strong magic?"

"Yes," said Belladonna, glaring at Steve. "But could you tell us what we need to free Branwyn?"

"Mugwyrt, attorlathe, stune--"

"Hang on," said Steve. "I've never heard of any of these."

"They'll be old names," said Belladonna. "We can look them up. Go on, please."

"Wegbrade, maethe, stithe, wergulu, fille, and finule," said Cradoe, as if he were reciting a familiar verse. "The others are herriff and lasar. All must be crushed to a paste, mixed with the juice of apples and poured around the perimeter of the place of binding."

"And you think this will work?"

"I do not. But perhaps it is worth the trying. She has been sitting in the marsh for a long time now."

"It's not actually a--"

"Thank you," said Belladonna, flashing Steve another glare. "We'll try our best."

"I must go now," said Cradoe, uneasily. "This place brings back too much pain, too much evil, too much sorrow."

"I'm sorry, old chap," said Elsie, patting him on the back. "It's a rum do, alright, but you've shown real pluck."

"What?" Cradoe stared at her, his miserable expression even more hangdog.

"She said we understand that this was difficult for you, and we admire your bravery," explained Belladonna.

"Seriously?" said Steve. "That was what she said? Have you got some kind of phrase-book?"

"I wish you luck," said Cradoe, in a way that made it clear that the only kind of luck he had ever encountered had been bad.

Belladonna started to thank him, but he had already vanished.

"Well done, Elsie," said Steve. "How on earth did you find him?"

"It was easy," said Elsie, smiling. "A friend told me that there are some people that never go to the parties. I guessed that he'd be one of them. Edward the Confessor never goes, so I just popped over to the House of Mists to ask him where Cradoe might be…and bobs-your-uncle!"

"That still leaves us with this list," said Belladonna, looking at the column of unfamiliar names.

"Maybe this will be one of the times when this stupid library is actually useful," said Steve. "What do you bet there's some old herbal or something here?"

"Let's split up," said Belladonna. "I'll take gardening. Steve and Elsie, you take history 'cause there's more of that."

For the next ten minutes, all was silent as they each scanned the shelves for anything that might be useful.

"Ha!" said Belladonna. "There's a book here called "The Complete Book of Herbs" and it's got pictures!"

She took the book over to one of the tables and was

soon joined by Steve with an old book on the languages of ancient Britain.

"Look," he said. "There's a glossary in the back." He pointed to a word. "Isn't that one of the herbs?"

Belladonna checked the list.

"Stune...yes!"

"It says here it's Lamb's Cress or Hairy Bittercress."

"Oh, it's not in the herb book."

"Uh oh."

"Wait," said Elsie. "I've heard of that. It's some kind of mustard. My grandmother used to add it to stews sometimes."

She ran over to the tiny food section, followed by Steve.

"There! Try that one!" she said, pointing at the oldest book on the shelf. "Look up stews or casseroles."

Steve did as he was told, and a smile slowly spread across his face.

"She's right. It looks like some kind of weed, though."

He showed the page to Belladonna, who sketched the plant as well as she could, and drew an arrow connecting it to the word.

"Let's start at the beginning," she said. "Mucgwyrt."

"That's got to be mugwort," said Steve.

Belladonna looked it up in the book. The picture showed a silvery-leafed shrub.

"I've seen that," she said, amazed that something so seemingly arcane could just be a common garden plant. "Our neighbors have a bush of it in their front garden. Okay, next is...attorlathe..."

"Betony," said Steve. "It says here that it used to be planted in churchyards to discourage ghosts."

"Honestly," laughed Elsie, "Why on earth would we want to hang around churchyards? The living really are daft sometimes!"

"I bet there's some in St. Abelard's," said Belladonna. "Aya should know it. Right...um...wegbrade."

"Hosta."

"Mrs. Naylor next door has some of those too – in the herbaceous border next to the mugwort."

"Jolly useful neighbor!" said Elsie.

"Maethe."

"Uh...chamomile."

Belladonna looked it up in the herb book.

"Yes! It looks sort of like a yellow daisy. Oh, it's what they use to make chamomile tea—I think my mum has some of that in the kitchen cupboard. Next...stithe."

"Nettle," read Steve. "Well, that's easy, there's a big patch of them over by the football pitch."

"Wergulu."

"Crab-apple."

"There's a tree in the garden of the convent next door," said Elsie. "I can see it from the attic. I think it's still got some fruit on it."

"How on earth are we going to get into a convent?" asked Steve.

"Over the wall, perhaps," suggested Elsie.

"Or maybe we could just ring the bell and ask them for some," said Belladonna, rolling her eyes. "Right... fille."

"Thyme. That's easy."

"Finule."

"Fennel. Yuck. Hate that stuff. Too aniseedy."

"Yes, but they'll have it at the shops. Okay, last two… herrif."

"Burdock."

"That's easy, too," said Elsie. "Burdock always grows near nettles."

"Last one – lasar."

"Laserpiciferis…oh."

"What?"

"It says here that it's extinct."

"It can't be," gasped Belladonna, grabbing the book off Steve, before frantically scanning the index in her herbs book.

"Maybe you can miss that one out," suggested Elsie.

"You know that won't work," said Steve. "If we've learned anything, it's that a single change to a potion completely alters what it does. Remember the manticore?"

"I wasn't actually there, but I get your point. It won't work, then, will it? We'll have to find another way."

"No, wait," said Belladonna. "It's extinct."

"Not getting your point, old thing," said Elsie.

"Extinct," repeated Belladonna. "Like dinosaurs and mammoths…and you."

"Wait…you think it might be growing in the Land of the Dead?"

"Why not? The Queen of the Abyss, Miss Parker, that is, said that everything that has ever lived and died was somewhere on the Other Side."

"You're joking, right?" said Steve. "You want us to go to the Other Side to find a plant we've never seen?"

"We don't even know what it looks like," said Elsie.

"We'll ask," said Belladonna. "Who wrote your book, Steve?"

"Ummm…Gertrude Jekyll."

"Is she dead?"

Steve flipped to the front of the book and scanned the biography.

"Yes. 1932. She was born in 1843. It says she was a really famous garden designer."

"Garden designer?" said Elsie. "Can I see?"

Steve stepped aside and turned the pages for her, as a smile spread slowly across her face.

"I know exactly where she'll be! See you there!"

"Wait," yelled Belladonna, stopping Elsie mid-dematerialization. "Why do we have to come? Can't you just bring it? We've got all these other things to find."

"If I bring it, it'll just vanish when I hand it to you. If it's going to exist in the Land of the Living, a living person has to fetch it."

Steve marched over to the Classics shelves, rearranged the books in alphabetical order and stood back as the door to the Sibyl's temple slid open.

"Come on," he said. "Let's get this done."

"But lunch is nearly over," complained Belladonna. "We'll miss all our afternoon classes!"

"Sometimes sacrifices have to be made."

3.
Gertrude Jekyll

"WE'RE GOING TO GET in so much trouble," muttered Belladonna, as she joined the grinning Steve by the door. "See you in a few minutes, Elsie."

"Righty-ho!"

"Um...could you go first?" asked Steve.

Belladonna rolled her eyes and took his key-ring flashlight.

"Honestly," she said. "I don't see how you can be so scared of leggy insects when you keep dropping spiders onto the chess club's boards."

"That's different. It isn't dark."

"That makes no sense," muttered Belladonna as they stepped through the door and started the descent.

Journeys usually feel shorter once you've done them a few times, but the aged winding staircase beneath the school library always felt never ending. Eventually, however, they arrived in the Cumaean Sibyl's temple. The torches on either side of the great stone chair sprang to life and the Sibyl's disembodied voice echoed around the chamber.

"WHO DARES TO…oh, it's you again."

"Yes, sorry," said Belladonna. "But we just need to use the lift."

"You don't need to know the future?"

"Not this time. Thanks, though," said Steve.

"Not even a little?" asked the Sibyl, rather plaintively. "I could tell you if it's going to rain tomorrow."

"We don't really need an oracle for that," said Steve, smiling. "Maybe next time."

"'Bye," said Belladonna. "Sorry."

"Typical," muttered the Sibyl.

"*Arate Thyras!*" commanded Belladonna.

"Oh, I see," complained the voice of the Sibyl, which had moved from the vicinity of the great stone chair to somewhere up in the ceiling near the stairs. "Now you know ancient Greek. Very clever."

The doors of the elevator slid open and Belladonna and Steve stepped inside. Steve pressed the now-familiar button for the Land of the Dead, and the lift shot off sideways, before descending rapidly at a slight angle and landing with a bump.

Belladonna said the ancient Greek for "open the doors" again and they found themselves back in the huge rotunda of the House of Mists, the home of the ghosts' seat of government, the Conclave of Shadow.

Elsie was waiting, but other than that, the building was strangely silent.

"Where is everyone?" asked Belladonna.

"Getting ready for Halloween," said Elsie. "Come on, she's in the garden."

She led they way out of the huge doors, across the pillared portico, and down to the garden that had so impressed Belladonna the first time she saw it, with its lawns and arbors, interlocking flower beds and meandering paths. It had been beautiful then, even though everything had been dead, but now it was simply glorious, the flowers and foliage cascading over each other in a riot of color and fragrance.

Elsie walked to the small pavilion in the center of the garden and tapped on the side of the open door.

"Hello?" she called, cautiously.

"Just a moment! I'm thinning a seedbox!" The voice was slightly husky and ridiculously posh, like people in old movies.

"I bet she's got secateurs," whispered Steve.

"Shh!"

"Ah, well now! What can I do for you?"

Even though Belladonna knew that the dead could choose to be any age they wanted, for some reason she had still been expecting a ninety year old woman. But the girl who stepped out into the sunlight was young and hearty, her cheeks flushed pink from working. She was wearing an elegant pale blue and white striped crinoline dress, but had hoisted the hem nearly up to her knees with yellow drawstrings knotted at her waist. On her feet were a pair of high button boots, somewhat muddy from working in the beds, while elegant gardening gloves protected her hands.

"Hello, Miss Jekyll," said Belladonna, shaking her hand.

"It's pronounced Jeekle, actually, but please just call me Gertrude."

"Really?" said Steve. "But what about 'Dr. Jekyll and Mr. Hyde?'"

"That is supposed to be pronounced Jeekle too, dear. Robert Louis Stevenson was a friend of my brother's, you see. So...young Elsie, here, tells me you're looking for a plant."

"Yes," said Belladonna, pleased that she wasn't going to have to explain the whole thing again. "It's called... um...hang on..."

She retrieved the list from her pocket and handed it to Gertrude.

"My goodness," she said. "What appalling handwriting you have. Don't they teach copperplate any more?"

"No," said Steve. "They're mostly pleased if we can string a few sentences together without saying 'axe,' 'like,' or 'y'know.'"

"Dear me. You'll be telling me we've lost the Empire, next."

"Well, actually--" began Steve.

"It's the last one," said Belladonna, hastily, digging Steve in the ribs.

"Laserpiciferis," read Gertrude. "Well, I've heard of it, of course, but it was extinct well before my time. Let's ask Seneca, he's up at the house."

"Really?" said Steve. "I thought everyone was getting ready for these parties we've been hearing so much about."

"Stoic philosophers don't go to parties, dear. Come along!"

She grabbed a large sun hat from a chair near the door, tied the ribbons under her chin, and marched back toward the house with Belladonna, Steve and Elsie running to catch up.

She finally stopped in the middle of the rotunda, and yelled: "Seneca!"

No reply.

"Come along, Seneca, I know you're here! It's Gertrude!"

A door creaked open near the stairs and a sour-faced man peered out.

"I don't care who it is. I'm not going to any blasted parties!"

"We're not trying to get you to go to a party, dear, we just want to know what a plant looked like."

"What plant?"

"Laserpiciferis," said Belladonna.

"Are you alive?" asked Seneca, looking her up and down.

"Yes."

"Well, it's extinct."

"We know that," said Steve. "We just want to know what it looked like."

"Humph," growled Seneca. "Wait here."

The door closed with a click that was followed by the sound of rummaging and things falling off shelves.

Then, just as Belladonna had decided he wasn't going to come back, the door creaked open again and Seneca thrust an unrolled scroll at Gertrude.

"That's it. The one on the left."

"Oh, I know where that is!" said Gertrude. "Thank you, Seneca. Come along everyone!"

And she was off again, out of the doors and down the garden.

"I wonder if she had this much energy when she was alive," muttered Steve.

"Probably," said Elsie. "She was telling me how many gardens she'd done. It made me tired just thinking about it."

They finally caught up with her at the far end of the garden in a sunny spot near a gurgling stream. Gertrude pointed to a clump of sturdy green plants near the water's edge.

"That's it," she said.

Belladonna bent down and started picking leaves.

"I don't think that's what you need, dear. I've read that the ancient Romans valued it for its resin. You'll need to cut through the stalk."

Belladonna tried pulling one of the plants out of the ground, but it didn't budge. Gertrude smiled, moved Belladonna gently aside, then reached into her pocket, took out a pair of clippers and went to work on the stalk.

"My goodness!" she said, stepping back. "That is a very tough plant!"

Belladonna turned and looked at Steve.

"This is so weird," he said, stepping forward and

taking the ruler out of his pocket. It instantly turned into the secateurs again. He leaned down and snipped through the stalk as if it were nothing more than a dandelion.

"Wait a minute," gasped Gertrude. "Is that the Rod of Gram?"

"Yes," said Steve, pocketing the ruler once again.

"So you're the Paladin? Then that must mean…"

"Yes," said Belladonna, a little sheepishly. "I'm the Spellbinder."

"Well, I never! What an honor! And in my garden, too!"

"Thanks for helping us," said Belladonna. "The garden is lovely."

"Not at all. I'll walk with you back to the lift."

She set off more slowly this time, showing off her garden and explaining her plantings and why she'd chosen the different flowers and shrubs. By the time they reached the House of Mists again, Belladonna was so enchanted with the tour that she'd almost forgotten why they'd come.

"Thank you so much," she said, really meaning it and shaking Gertrude's hand.

"Not at all. You must go and see some of my gardens. I believe quite a few still exist."

"We will."

Elsie pushed the button for the elevator and the doors slid open.

"See you later!"

4.

Spells and Sprites

A S USUAL, THE ELEVATOR didn't return them to the oracle, but to the groundsman's shed near the football pitch. It was almost completely dark, but they were able to find the nettles and burdock with Steve's flashlight. Belladonna wrapped the stinging nettles in a tissue from her pocket and they returned to the school to retrieve their coats and bags, which they managed to do without being caught, much to their amazement.

"There must be a staff meeting or something," said Steve, as they slipped outside and walked up the steps to the convent.

Belladonna rang the doorbell, which was answered by a rather surprised nun. Steve explained that they needed some crabapples for a class project and that someone had told them the convent had a tree.

"We were wondering if we could have a few?"

"Why, certainly," said the nun.

She asked them to step inside, then disappeared down a long corridor, reappearing a moment later, from a completely different direction, with a small plastic bag of crabapples.

"Will that be enough?"

"Yes," said Belladonna, smiling. "Thank you very much!"

They picked up the rest of the herbs on the way back to Lychgate Lane, buying the fennel and apple juice at the green grocers, and plucking a few leaves of mugwort and hosta from the garden next door.

"I'm home!" yelled Belladonna as they walked into the house. "Steve is here!"

"Hello, Steve!" said Mr. Johnson cheerily as he floated an inch or two above his easy chair, watching the news. "Are you staying for dinner?"

"No thanks," said Steve. "I promised I'd help dad in the shop. The Christmas stuff will be in soon and we need to make room."

"We've just come to make a potion."

"Splendid. Your grandmother's in the kitchen, I know she'd love to help with that."

Of course, Grandma Johnson was thrilled, and soon had the kitchen counters festooned with bowls, spoons, whisks and a pestle and mortar.

"Um…Actually, I think the food processor might work best," said Belladonna.

"But where's the fun in that? Come on now, let's get mixing!"

Belladonna got the chamomile and dried thyme out of the cupboard and added it to everything else, while Steve poured some of the apple juice over the whole lot until they had a kind of muddy liquid.

"Right," said Grandma Johnson. "That smells suitably vile. I gather this is something to do with the bog girl you met yesterday?"

"Yes," said Belladonna. "Her uncle said the Spirits of the Black Water don't really need a blood binding. He said this might work instead."

"The operative word being 'might,'" said Steve. "I've never met such a miserable bloke in all my life."

"Well, he *was* needlessly sacrificed in a swamp, Stephen," said Grandma Johnson. "I can see how that might color your outlook. So what do you have to do with it? Smear it on a tree or something?"

"No. I think we need to sort of pour it around the area where they are going to be bound."

"Ah, I see. A little more apple juice, I think, then, Steve."

Steve poured and stirred while Grandma Johnson searched through the cupboards, eventually producing one of the plastic bottles that Belladonna's mum used for drizzling sauces.

Belladonna poured it in, screwed on the top and pushed the cap onto the nozzle.

"Where is it you're going?" asked Grandma Johnson, putting the bottle into the fridge.

"The Roman fort near Hegland Moss," said Steve.

"That's quite a long way. I'd drive you, but I've got clients all day tomorrow. There's always a rush at Halloween. We'd better ask your dad."

They trooped into the living room and explained the

45

problem. Mr. Johnson turned the sound down on the television, thought for a moment and then started going on about A-roads and turning at lights.

"No, no," said Grandma Johnson, a little impatiently. "They're thirteen. Bus routes. They need bus routes."

"Oh, right. Um...are you sure this is entirely safe? What if it goes wrong and you both die? I'll never hear the end of it from your mum, I can tell you!"

"Of course it's safe," lied Steve. "I mean, they're already bound, aren't they? We're just going to sort of double-bind them so that Branwyn can leave and go to the Other Side."

"She's been sitting there soaking wet for nearly two thousand years, dad," said Belladonna, hoping that he wasn't going to have one of those "responsible parent" moments.

"That is pretty unpleasant, I must admit," he said, thoughtfully. "I'll tell you what, so long as you both go first thing and promise to get back before dark, I just won't mention it to your mum. Deal?"

"Deal," said Steve and Belladonna in unison.

"Thanks, dad."

"Okay, so...buses...I'd say the 25 to Staple Street, then the 61. That'll drop you in Grafton village, then it's just a short walk. Daylight, though, right? No lingering!"

"Promise!"

Belladonna walked Steve out to the door.

"Your dad is ace. Mine would never let me do anything like this, particularly since mum left. I never tell him anything I'm doing."

"Dad and Grandma Johnson are completely irresponsible," explained Belladonna, smiling. "Mum's going to kill him when she finds out."

"He's already dead."

"You don't know mum," said Belladonna, grinning.

She watched Steve walk down the path and away down the street. It was strange to think that she was going to spend her evening in front of the fire, watching TV and talking to her dad and grandma while Steve would be spending his helping to clear out a storeroom in a freezing shop.

"Staunchly Springs" had just ended (with the startling revelation that George's half-brother, Phil, was actually his mother's best friend's grandmother's sister's child and his real name was Francine), when Belladonna suddenly jumped to her feet.

"We forgot one!"

"Heaven's, Belladonna!" gasped Grandma Johnson. "You nearly gave me a heart attack!"

"You forgot one what?" asked her dad.

"One of the herbs. Betony. It's supposed to grow in church yards. We were going to check St. Abelard's but I forgot."

Her dad looked at his mother and sighed.

"Well, I can't leave the house," he said. "And there's no way she's going alone in the dark."

Grandma Johnson heaved herself to her feet.

"Come on then," she said. "Let's make it quick before "Great British Bake Off" starts."

47

Belladonna threw on her jacket and grabbed a flashlight, then waited impatiently while Grandma Johnson wound a long woolen scarf three times around her neck, fastened her coat right up to the top, pulled on a hat, put on her gloves and picked up her umbrella.

"It's not the Arctic, grandma!"

"When you get to my age, you chill easily. Now come on."

They walked down Lychgate Lane to the church, with Grandma Johnson admiring the houses that had put up Halloween decorations and tut-tutting the ones that hadn't.

"Some people are just party-poopers," she muttered.

Belladonna stopped across the street from the church. She couldn't risk taking her grandmother in and frightening off the charnel sprites, so she convinced her to wait, turned on the flashlight and walked into the wet and weedy churchyard alone.

"Aya!" she called, as loud as she dared. "Aya! Are you here?"

"Of course I'm here!" said a familiar voice right behind her. "Charnel sprites love Halloween."

"Let me guess," said Belladonna, turning around and lowering the flashlight to charnel sprite height. "Parties?"

"Absolutely," said Aya, enthusiastically, her slightly purple skin shimmering in the light. "Wouldn't miss it for the world. It's like old home week. What are you doing here at this time of night? Not calling the Hunt again, I hope."

"I need some betony," explained Belladonna. "I read that they used to plant it in graveyards to discourage ghosts."

"Silly humans," giggled Aya. "There's some over here."

Belladonna followed the charnel sprite to the far side of the church and picked some leaves of the missing ingredient.

"Are you making the Nine Herbs Charm?"

"Sort of," said Belladonna. "But with two more to make eleven. It's for a binding."

She explained about Branwyn and the Spirits of the Black Water.

"Ugh," said Aya, shuddering. "Old Magic. Branwyn won't know the way to the Other Side, though. I'll make sure our local office sends someone."

"Thanks. I didn't know you had regional charnel sprite offices."

"Of course we do! How else could we manage? You lot are constantly popping off."

Belladonna smiled, thanked Aya again, and returned to her grandmother. It was the semi-final of "Great British Bake Off," which Grandma Johnson wouldn't dream of missing, so it was nearly bed time before they were able to add the betony to the binding potion.

"So much for an early night," said Belladonna.

"Don't worry," said her dad. "I'll make sure you're up in time."

She blew him a kiss goodnight, gave her grandma a hug and headed upstairs to bed. She was tired, but sleep wouldn't come. Tomorrow would be something different, it wasn't going to be about the Words or anything to do with being the Spellbinder, really. It was about Old Magic and she wasn't sure how it would work or even if it would do anything at all. She didn't even know anything about the spirits they were trying to bind. What if they made it worse and released them by mistake? She kept wishing that Miss Parker was around. But then maybe she'd say the same thing as Mrs. Jay—that some things can't be fixed.

That was probably true, but Belladonna couldn't help feeling that the least a person could do was try.

5.

The Binding

THE NEXT MORNING WAS overcast but dry, and really cold. Belladonna bundled up, wore two pairs of socks, sturdy boots, carefully packed the potion into her pink backpack and headed out to the bus stop. Steve was already there, wearing a combat jacket over his hoody, though his hair looked like it hadn't seen a comb in weeks and there were dark circles under his eyes.

"Did you get any sleep at all?" asked Belladonna.

"Not much. There was some zombie movie on when my dad and me got home, so we watched it. I think I got about two hours."

Belladonna rolled her eyes and was about to say something about taking things seriously, when the bus arrived. She had expected it to be full of people with the kind of miserable expressions almost exclusive to those who have to get up on a Saturday to go to work, but everyone seemed remarkably cheerful. They were chatting to each other and pointing out landmarks and scenery and generally having a good time. There were no empty seats left, though, so she and Steve had to stand.

At the next stop a man with what seemed to be a heavy case got on. He hesitated near the front, gave Belladonna and Steve a funny look, then inched past them and sat down.

In a seat occupied by someone else.

Belladonna stared as the ghost rolled its eyes and stood up. Two other ghosts made room on their seat and the displaced phantom squeezed in.

"Are they all…," whispered Steve. "I mean…except that guy, obviously… but are they all…dead?"

"I…guess," said Belladonna.

They watched in silence for the next two stops as some ghosts got off and others got on.

"You've been seeing them longer than I have," said Steve, finally. "Have you ever seen this many in one place?"

"Never."

They got off at Staple Street, crossed the road and waited for the number 61 bus.

"They're everywhere," said Belladonna. "Look over there."

Staple Street was a busy shopping street and there were plenty of people walking up and down and in and out of shops, but for every living person, there seemed to be two or three ghosts.

"Is this because it's Halloween?" said Steve.

"I suppose. But I've never seen this before."

"Well, Elsie said they didn't celebrate last year. How long have you been able to see them?"

"About three years."

"Were your parents...I mean...were they...you know...when..."

"Yes," said Belladonna, smiling at Steve's efforts to avoid using the words "alive" or "dead."

"So that would explain it, wouldn't it? I mean you'd be at home with them."

"It started sort of gradually. I couldn't see all the ghosts at first, just a few. So I probably wouldn't have noticed. And sometimes it's really hard to tell who's alive and who's dead."

"That's the really weird part," said Steve, as the 61 bus pulled up. "You'd think it would be obvious."

The second bus wasn't as crowded, though there was an Elizabethan lady with a Victorian gentleman sitting together near the back.

Belladonna and Steve got off in Grafton village, which was quite pretty and featured large helpful signs directing them to the Roman fort. After a fifteen minute walk they arrived in the parking lot and stopped. There were ghosts wandering all over the ruins, some looked like Roman soldiers, visiting their old workplace, while others were from all sorts of different periods in history and seemed to be tourists. The whole effect was like a costume party.

"D'you think they'll notice?"

"I don't know," said Belladonna. "I don't suppose it matters..."

"No," said Steve. "Are you ready?"

"I suppose so," said Belladonna, tucking her hair behind her ears and taking the bottle out of her bag.

"Cool. Let's go…hang on…who's that?"

Belladonna looked over toward the parade ground. Branwyn was still sitting on the railway ties, still soaking wet even though the day was dry, but there was someone else with her, sitting close and talking up a storm, if the bobbing of her head was anything to go by.

"It can't be…" said Steve, as they walked closer.

"Hello, chaps!"

"Elsie! It's because of Halloween, right?"

"Yes," said Elsie. "It's the one day of the year we can go anywhere we like. I thought you might need a hand."

"Elsie's been telling me everything that's happened in history since I…came here," whispered Branwyn, happily.

"Well, not everything," said Elsie, a little sheepishly. "Just the good stuff. The best battles and the really interesting kings and queens. Oh, and trains and cars and gramophones, that sort of thing."

"I bet the British Empire got a mention, as well," said Belladonna, smiling.

"Or three or four," added Steve.

"I just can't believe the world is so big," said Branwyn. "So many other countries and all sorts of different people."

"Well, let's get you out of here so you can see it," said Belladonna. "Or the version on the Other Side, at least."

She put her backpack down and handed the bottle to Steve, then she closed her eyes and let the Words come.

"*Igi si gar!*" Reveal yourself! "*Igi si gar!*"

Even with her eyes closed, Belladonna could tell that

the Spirits of the Black Water had materialized. The intense wave of menace and hatred was almost palpable, like a punch to the stomach.

She opened her eyes and looked at the black swirling clouds. The other ghosts had noticed too, and were all standing stock still, and staring.

"What do we do?" asked Steve, trying to ignore the audience. "Just pour it around them?"

"I had a word with a Druid last night," said Elsie. "Took for-bally-ever to find the chap. He was a bit unwilling to talk because he was on his way to Stonehenge and kept going on about being late for the sunrise."

"I thought Stonehenge didn't have anything to do with druids," said Steve.

"It doesn't," said Elsie. "It's just a really good place for a party, apparently. Anyway, he said in order to free the blood binding, the new one has to be inside the old."

"Great. Anything else?"

"You have to recite the ingredients over and over until the binding is complete."

"Please tell me you brought the list," said Steve.

Belladonna rummaged through her backpack and held the list aloft, triumphantly.

"I imagine it has to be the old names," she said.

"I should think so," said Elsie, leaning over her shoulder. "And I should think the order is important, too."

"Right," said Belladonna. "Who's going to do what?"

"I think Steve should pour the potion," said Elsie. "He can run the fastest. After all, he's on the under-15 footie team now."

"I am?"

"They put the notice up yesterday afternoon. We were all on the Other Side."

"Aceballs!"

"Okay," said Belladonna. "That means you and I will recite the list, Elsie."

"I'll help," said Elsie, smiling. "But I think it's the living person who counts."

"So all that's left is to find out where the old binding line was."

All eyes turned to Branwyn.

"Do you remember?" asked Belladonna.

She had an awful feeling that the limits of the old binding might have been connected to items on the landscape when Hegland Moss had been a marsh, all of which would be long gone now.

"Of course I do," whispered Branwyn. "How could I not? This is the western corner. It goes from here up to that oak just beyond the parade ground, then over to the remains of the watchtower, there, then back down to those bins and then here."

"Okay," said Steve. "So if I run the perimeter of the parade ground I should be well inside the old binding, right?"

"They'll be very angry," said Branwyn.

"Um…angry?"

"Yes."

"What do they do when they're angry?" asked Steve.

"They make you fear things," whispered Branwyn. "It's terrible…terrible."

"You do realize that you're not helping? A bit of optimism would be nice right about now."

"Oh, there's something else," announced Elsie.

"Of course there is," said Steve. "There's *always* something else. Do we have to do it backward on one foot or something?"

"No," said Belladonna, suddenly understanding. "We can't stop."

"How did you know that?" asked Elsie.

"I don't know...I just do. It's all part of the binding: the potion, the words...and the running."

"That'll be more Spellbinder hoodoo," said Steve. "Let's get on with it. Is everyone ready?"

"Thank you for trying," whispered Branwyn. "I want you to know...even if it doesn't work."

Belladonna smiled, stood next to Elsie and looked over at Steve, who had taken off his jacket and hoody and stood, shivering, bottle in hand.

"On three," he said, grimly. "One...two...THREE!!"

He took off up the right hand side of the parade ground, the herb mixture pouring from the nozzle of the sauce bottle as he went.

"Mucgwyrt, attorlathe, stune, wegbrade, maethe, stithe, wergulu, fille, finule, herrif, laserpiciferis, mucgwyrt, attorlathe..."

"They know! They know!" Branwyn was on her feet, terror in her eyes.

"...stune, wegbrade, stithe, wergulu..."

The spinning, folding, forming and reforming clouds had changed. Suddenly they seemed to have purpose—

two combined and shot across the parade ground toward Steve, who had just rounded the first corner, while another became solid and stretched itself into a black wall in front of Belladonna and Elsie. For a moment it just hung there, suspended in the air like a movie screen, but then it began to throb and started screaming and roaring at the volume a jet engine would have if you were actually *inside* the engine.

But it wasn't just noise, it was fear, oozing through the air like syrup, engulfing her, creeping into all the places in her mind where she had hidden the things that made her nervous, or made her scared and escalating every one of those feelings to the level of blind terror. She couldn't hear her own voice any more, and panic was all she could feel, but she kept going.

"…fille, finule, herrif, laserpiciferis, mucgwyrt…"

On the other side of the parade ground she could just make out Steve and the other Spirits of the Black Water. They seemed to be trying to entangle him in inky tendrils. Once he almost tripped, and then seemed to choke as shadowy fingers encircled his neck. As he turned the corner near the remains of the old watchtower, Belladonna could see tears on his cheeks, but a look of grim determination on his face. She wondered what the spirits had found inside his head, the thing that he most feared.

"…attorlathe, stune, wegbrade, maethe…"

Branwyn staggered and sat, her hands over her face and her body heaving with sobs. It didn't take any leap of imagination to know what fear the spirits had found within her, but Elsie stood fast, repeating the words with

Belladonna, attempting an encouraging smile, but not quite managing.

"…stithe, wergulu, fille, finule, herrif…"

Out of the corner of her eye, Belladonna could see that the ghosts from the ruins were converging on the parking lot. One man, with patterns dyed on his skin like Cradoe, separated himself from the crowd and walked up to her.

"Is it a binding?"

Belladonna nodded, but didn't stop. The man stepped away respectfully and rejoined the other ghosts.

"…laserpiciferis, mucgwyrt…"

Steve stumbled again, but didn't fall. He rounded the final corner, the Spirits of the Black Water had enveloped his body, and were grasping and writhing so that his face was the only part of him still visible. Belladonna could see his jaw tighten as he sprinted the last few yards as the final drips of the binding potion fell from the bottle and joined the first. He dropped to the ground, gasping and coughing. The binding should have been complete, yet still the shadows screamed. Belladonna knew she couldn't stop speaking.

"…attorlathe, stune…"

Steve rolled over.

"Why hasn't it worked?" His voice was a rasping gasp.

"You must bind it," whispered Branwyn, her voice barely audible. "You must bind it."

"…wegbrade, maethe, stune…"

Belladonna stopped. Mrs. Jay had been wrong, this

did need the Spellbinder. It *did* need Words of Power, just not ancient Sumerian ones. It needed English words. English words to imprison the worst of the Old Magic of England in this ground forever.

"This is a seal of the Old Times," she yelled, each word coming faster than the one before. "A vexation to fear, a mortification to pain, a shackle to disease and despair. It has power against three and against thirty, against the hand of a fiend and the spell of vile creatures. It has might against the onflying, it binds you here until the seas slip apart, until the sky falls away, until the earth beneath the feet of men turns to salt. This spell is bound, the Spirits of the Black Water are bound, the ground beneath them is bound, the air above them is bound. All is bound and will not be undone. By the power of Nantosuelta, who is the Queen of the Abyss, and the power of the Spellbinder, you shall move not, live not, die not!"

She stopped. That was all. She hoped it was all…that it was enough. She could sense Steve and Elsie staring at her, their mouths hanging open, and she could feel the crowd of ghosts watching and waiting behind her, but she didn't dare take her eyes off the Spirits of the Black Waters.

The screaming stopped first. Then the roaring whine that had followed Steve around the parade ground. Then the spirits themselves split apart and flew, swirling into the sky, only to recombine and like an arrow shoot towards the ground, vanishing beneath the muddy grass with a mighty groan.

The crowd of ghosts cheered and applauded.

"That was amazing," said a man in a smart suit.

"Fantastic," enthused a 1920s Flapper, the fringe on her dress swaying as she ran to congratulate the live girl.

"You must be a mighty seer to your people," said the man who had asked about the binding.

"Thank you," said Belladonna, suddenly feeling very shy. "It was nothing. Steve had the hard part."

"Best Halloween *ever*," said a girl who looked an awful lot like Jane Austen.

"Seriously, Belladonna," said Steve, scrambling to his feet, "that was even better than the standing stones thing!"

"It would've been better with a few "thees" and "thous," though," said Elsie. "Maybe a "begone" or two as well. More Shakespearian."

"But I'm not Shakespeare," said Belladonna, feeling a tiny bit deflated.

"Well, thank goodness for that," said Steve, laughing. "I wouldn't have understood a word you said!"

The crowd were still talking and laughing when a small voice broke through the cacophony.

"I'm free."

Belladonna whirled around. For a moment she'd forgotten why they were there. It was for Branwyn, the girl who had been sacrificed, who had spent two thousand years, wet and muddy and protecting the world from the Spirits of the Black Water.

She was still sitting on the railway tie, but the mud and water had gone. She was holding her hands up and staring at them. Staring at the pale skin she must have forgotten she ever had. She turned to Belladonna, her face flushing with joy and her eyes a sparkling blue. The linen dress was white again and the flowers fresh in her hair, which turned out to be light brown, not red at all.

She stood up and flung herself at Belladonna, but fell right through her.

"You're free," explained Elsie. "Not alive."

"I don't care. I don't care. This is…how do I get to…to…"

"Um…actually, I don't know," said Elsie. "I seem to remember someone helped me. I'm not sure how it's done. Not the first time."

She looked toward the crowd expectantly.

"A charnel sprite showed me the way," said the smart-suited man.

"Me too," said the Flapper.

Most of the others agreed and started discussing their own experiences, and how nice it was to get some tea and cake and relax a bit underground with the charnel sprites after all the fuss of their funerals.

They were still comparing notes when the bushes next to the parking lot started rustling and a small purplish man stepped out onto the gravel. Silence fell over the crowd.

"Perhaps I can be of help," said the purpleish man. "I received word from regional head office that there might be someone in need of a guide for the initial journey."

"Yes," said Belladonna, stepping forward. "That was Aya. We spoke last night."

"Oh, right," said Steve, "and I was the one who stayed

up too late."

"I visited the graveyard for five minutes, I didn't stay up all night watching a zombie flick!"

"What's…I mean who…?" Branwen was staring at the newcomer, confused and a little worried.

"This is…I'm sorry, I don't know your name," said Belladonna, anxious to do things properly.

"I am Nolo, and I will be your charnel sprite."

"This is Branwyn," said Belladonna. "She's been waiting for two thousand years."

"Well, then, we'd better get going," said Nolo. "It is my job to show you the way to the Other Side, young lady. Unless you'd prefer to stay for a party? There are a great many of them tonight, you know."

"Does the sun shine on the Other Side?"

"Almost all the time, I believe."

"Then I'd like to go. I'd like to be warm again." She turned to Belladonna and Steve. "Thank you. Thank you both. I didn't think it would work. But…oh, I wish I could touch you!"

"Perhaps you'll meet again," said Elsie, helpfully. "When they're over on our side, you can hug to your heart's content…if you're that sort of person. It's not very British, you know, all that display of emotion."

Branwyn smiled.

"I don't care," she said. "I've waited a long time."

Nolo held out his hand and led Branwyn gently back toward the bushes. She glanced back, her eyes shining.

"Goodbye! And thank you. Thank you all!"

The crowd of ghosts applauded again, then started

wandering away in small groups, still chatting excitedly about what they'd just seen. Belladonna watched until Branwyn and Nolo had vanished into the thicket, then picked up her backpack and turned back to Steve and Elsie. Steve brushed himself off and shrugged on his jacket.

"Right," said Elsie. "Shall we go?"

"Go?" said Steve. "Where?"

"Why to Belladonna's house, of course."

"My house? What for?"

"Well, partly because I've never seen it and it's Halloween, so I can," said Elsie. "But mostly for the party."

"What party?"

"Oh, you are dense! The party your mother's been planning for months."

"So that's why she hasn't been home so much?"

"I think this might be a 'duh' moment, Belladonna," said Steve, grinning.

"Did you know?"

"No, of course not. But it makes sense. Come on, I think there's a bus in a few minutes."

"A bus?" said Elsie, excitedly. "An omnibus? Oh, how spiffing! My parents would never use them. They said they were--"

"Yes, we know," said Belladonna and Steve, laughing. "*Vulgar.*"

Made in the USA
Charleston, SC
05 February 2014